MICHAEL DAHL

# CROSS GODS

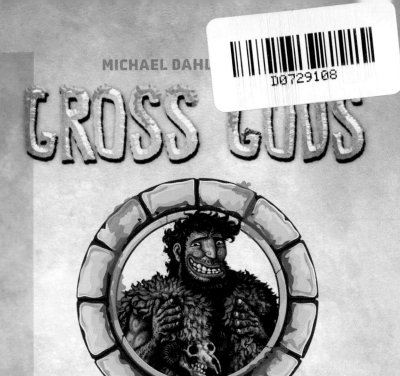

## JASON and the Totally FUNKY FLEECE

BY BLAKE HOENA

ILLUSTRATED BY IVICA STEVANOVIC

STONE ARCH BOOKS
a capstone imprint

Gross Gods is published by
Stone Arch Books
A Capstone Imprint
1710 Roe Crest Drive
North Mankato, Minnesota 56003
www.capstonepub.com

Library of Congress Cataloging-in-Publication Data
Hoena, B. A., author.
Title: Jason and the totally funky fleece / by Blake Hoena .
Description: North Mankato, Minnesota : Stone Arch Books, a
        Capstone imprint, [2020] | Series: Michael Dahl presents: Gross
        gods | Summary: In this humorous (and gross) retelling of the
        classic Greek myth, Jason sets out to retrieve the funky royal
        fleece which his father, king of Iolcus, lost in a bet—but the
        heroes of Greece may not be able to stand the smell long
        enough to get it back from Colchis.
Identifiers: LCCN 2019006160| ISBN 9781496583604 (hardcover) |
        9781496584618 (pbk.) | ISBN 9781496583659 (ebook PDF)
Subjects: LCSH: Jason (Mythological character)—Juvenile fiction. |
        Argonauts (Greek mythology)—Juvenile fiction. | Mythology,
        Greek—Juvenile fiction. | Quests (Expeditions)—Juvenile
        fiction. | Humorous stories. | CYAC: Humorous stories. | Argonauts
        (Greek mythology)—Fiction. | Mythology, Greek—Fiction. |
        LCGFT: Mythological fiction. | Humorous fiction .
Classification: LCC PZ7.H67127 Jas 2019 | DDC 813.6 [Fic]—dc23
LC record available at https://lccn.loc.gov/2019006160

Design Elements: Shutterstock: Andrii_M, Anna Violet, Nikolai Zaburdaev

Designer: Tracy McCabe
Production Designer: Tori Abraham

Printed in the United States of America.
PA70

# MICHAEL
# DAHL
# PRESENTS

Michael Dahl has written about werewolves, magicians, and superheroes. He loves funny books, scary books, and mysterious books. Every Michael Dahl Presents book is chosen by Michael himself and written by an author he loves. The books are about favorite subjects like legendary myths, haunted houses, farting pigs, or magical powers that go haywire. Read on!

# FROM MICHAEL DAHL:

Dear Reader,

When I was a kid, every Saturday at noon I watched "Epic Theater." I wouldn't brush my teeth or take a shower until I had watched an adventure about the secret Sons of Hercules. Hey, I thought, maybe I was a Greek hero in disguise and didn't know it! No such luck. No Medusa showed up at my door, no Hydra terrorized the neighborhood. So, I read every book on mythology in our school library, just in case Zeus sent me on a quest. But then I ran out of stories.

Recently, I asked some terrific authors I know to tell new adventures. They retell the exploits of my favorite heroes, like Hercules and Perseus and Jason, but in a totally different way. A gross and gruesome and disgusting way! Crack open a book from GROSS GODS, and you'll be inspired to be an epic hero. You might also be inspired to take a shower and clean the gunk from between your toes.

READ ON!

*Michael Dahl*

# TABLE OF CONTENTS

## CHAPTER ONE

# THE LOST FLEECE

Jason stomps through the city of Iolcus. He is mad. Angry. Fuming hot, like a dragon's breath pepper. Peppers so spicy, they burn—literally. If you eat one, actual flames will shoot out of your actual butt.

THAT is how mad our hero is!

Jason enters the palace. He storms down a hallway with his footsteps *CLOMP! CLOMP! CLOMPING!*

He is angry because his father, the king, has been thrown in jail. The worst part? His uncle, Pelias, put him there.

Jason barges into the throne room.

"I need to speak with you, Pelias!" Jason shouts.

As he stands in the middle of the room, his stomach begins to gurgle. Not from eating a dragon's breath pepper—no—but from being nervous and a little bit scared. Whenever that happens, his stomach rumbles and grumbles.

Sometimes when he's really afraid, he even—*PHHHTTTBBB!*

"Do you need to use the restroom?" Pelias asks, wrinkling his nose at his nephew's sour fart.

"No!" Jason exclaims. "That's not why I'm here!"

Jason's stomach continues to make all sorts of noises. But he is not afraid of his uncle. Pelias is a weaselly little guy with a whiskery mustache. The guards next to him are another story. They have lowered long pointy spears at Jason.

Our hero is deathly allergic to pointy things, especially when they are pointed at him. **PFFFTTT!** He toots.

"Are you sure?" his uncle asks.

"No! I want to know why you threw my father in jail," Jason demands.

"Because he lost the royal fleece," his uncle replies.

Most rulers wear gold crowns as a sign of their power. Others have bejeweled staffs. But not the rulers of Iolcus. They wear a robe called a fleece. It is not golden or covered in jewels or special in anyway.

Actually, the fleece is kind of old and funky smelling, like a wet dog that has rolled around is something super stinky. It is made of the wool from a ram his great-great-great grandfather once owned.

"It was an accident," Jason says.

It really wasn't. His father had challenged King Aeetes of Colchis to a burping contest. And his father let loose such a ginormous belch that he passed out from lack of oxygen. King Aeetes then stole the fleece.

"That's no excuse," Pelias says.

Jason wishes he could just kick his uncle off of the throne, but the guards continue to point their long, pointing spears at him. And that causes his stomach to warble and garble.

Jason lets out another *PTTTHHHBBB!*

"Are you sure you don't need to use the restroom?" his uncle asks again.

"No!" Jason shouts. "I just want my father, the king, released from prison."

"Not without the fleece," Pelias says.

"Then fine! I will get it back!" Jason exclaims.

He spins around to leave, but not before letting loose another **PTTTHHHBBB!** and a little **PFFT!** for good measure.

"And maybe I will hit the can on the way out!" Jason shouts as he walks out of the throne room.

## CHAPTER TWO

# SETTING SAIL

While sitting on the toilet, Jason thinks and *PTTTHHHBBBS!* He wonders and he *PFFFTS!*

He is not sure how he will get the fleece back. Colchis is far, far away.

There will be dangers. *PFFFT!*

Maybe monsters. *PTTTHHH!*

All the thinking and wondering about such things only upsets his stomach further.

## PFFFTTTHHHBBBSSS!

Our hero will need help with his quest, so he sends for his friends. They are some of the greatest heroes in all of Greece.

First, Hercules arrives. He is the strongest man alive, and he likes to brag about it. As he struts down the streets of Iolcus, he puffs out his chest and flexes his biceps.

"I am the mighty Hercules!" he boasts.

Next comes Theseus, who is a bit clumsy. As he walks down the streets of Iolcus, he trips and **SPLATS!** He falls face-first into a pile of manure.

"Who pooped in the middle of the road?" Theseus moans. He licks his lips. "Tastes like cow. Or horse! Yes, definitely horse."

Then Perseus shows up. He is often forgetful. As he walks down the street, he looks down at his pants.

*Did I change my underwear today?* he wonders.

Lastly, his friend Odysseus arrives. He thinks he is supersmart. He rows into the city's harbor in a tiny boat and ties his craft to the dock.

"I brought a ship!" he says, and then he pulls out a sheet of toilet paper with some writing on it. "And a map!"

"That looks more like a dingy than a ship," Theseus says.

"Yeah, it's pretty small," Perseus adds.

"Do you think we'll all fit?" Hercules wonders aloud.

"I call the stern!" Jason shouts as he jumps into the back of the boat.

He grabs the rudder while his friends each grab an oar.

"Row!" Jason shouts at his friends.

They pull on the oars, and the boat lurches forward.

"Row!" Jason repeats.

His friends swing the oars forward and pull again.

*"Row your boat!"* Jason sings.

The heroes are off to Colchis. But they are also hoping to have some fun along the way.

"We are bound to have exciting adventures," Odysseus says.

"I hope we find monstcrs to slay," Theseus adds.

"And beasts to battle," Odysseus says.

"I will slay more monsters and battle more beasts than all of you!" Hercules brags.

The thought of monsters and beasts only makes Jason's stomach rumble and grumble.

Jason is thankful that he is sitting at the back of the boat when he starts to **PFFFT!** and **PTTTHHHB!**

For days, the heroes row on. At one point, they sail near an island. A cyclops stands atop the island's highest peak and hurls boulders at them.

**SPLOOSH!**

"Let's go battle him!" Theseus says.

**SPLASH!**

"I could use the exercise," Hercules says, flexing his biceps.

**SPLUSH!**

As Jason feels the gurgling in his stomach, he steers the ship away from the island with a **PTTTHHHB!**

"Our quest is to get the fleece," Jason says. "Not battle a cyclops."

Another time, they sail past a rocky shore where a group of Amazons stand. These warrior women hit their spears against their shields. **CLANK! CLANK! CLANK!**

"Come fight us?" one shouts.

"We won't hurt you too badly," another yells out.

"Are you heroes?" yet another calls. "Or are you *zeroes*?"

Jason's friends turn to him. He feels his stomach begin to gurgle, and a little **PFFT!** sneaks out. He is not sure if he is more afraid of the Amazons **CLANKING** their shields or his friends glaring at him.

"Our quest is to get the fleece," Jason says. "Not battle Amazons."

"But they are challenging us," Theseus points out.

"I'm not a zero," Perseus pouts.

"Can't that smelly fleece wait?" Odysseus wonders aloud.

But Jason steers past the rocky shore. The heroes sail by roaring monsters and howling beasts. They sail around islands of armored warriors and a land full of giant scorpions.

"This is *sooOOOooOOoo* boring," Hercules whines.

# CHAPTER THREE

# FOOD FIGHT!

Finally, Jason sees land up ahead with no raging beasts or scary monsters.

"Where are we?" Jason asks. "I see a castle atop that hill."

"This is the kingdom of Salmydessus," Odysseus says, looking at his map. "And that's where King Phineas lives."

"Let's go see if we can get some supplies from him," Jason says. "Our stores of food and water are running low."

"And Hercules used the last of the toilet paper two days ago," Theseus says.

"Yeah, I've had to use Odysseus' map to wipe," Perseus adds. "Twice."

**"EEEWWWW!"** Odysseus groans, sniffing his map.

Jason and his friends tie the boat up to a dock. Then they march up the hill toward the castles.

What they find surprises them. The castle is in ruins. Windows are shattered. Holes have been punched through the roof. Stones crumble away from the walls.

Inside, things are even worse. Smashed furniture is scattered across the floor. Paintings are ripped to shreds. Streaks of dirt cover the walls and floor and ceiling.

"And what's that smell?" Odysseus asks.

"It smells worse than Jason after chili night," Theseus adds.

"That's not my fault! You need stop adding dragon's breath peppers to it," Jason says.

"Yeah," Perseus adds. "It feels like I'm farting fire after eating one of those."

The heroes continue to explore. They do not find King Phineas until entering the dining hall. Here, the mess is the worst. Piles of rotting, smelly, fly-infested food lie everywhere.

"Is anyone here?" Jason asks.

"Wh-wh-who's there?" a squeaky voice replies. An elderly man pokes his head out from under a table.

"King Phineas, is that you?" Jason asks.

"It is," the king says. "And who are you?"

Jason quickly introduces himself and his hero friends.

"We are on our way to Colchis to get my father's fleece," Jason adds.

"But what happened here?" Perseus asks.

"Your castle is a pigsty!" Hercules says.

"Worse," Odysseus says. "Pigs would be embarrassed to live here."

"It's because of the harpies," the king says.

"Harpies?" Jason asks.

"Yes, I invited them to dinner," the king exclaims. "And they won't leave. What's worse, those foul bird ladies have horrible manners."

Just then, the dinner bell sounds.

**DING! DONG! DING!**

"Oh no," the king says, ducking back under the table. "They're back for seconds."

A moment later, servants enter with trays of food. All of it is set out on some tables.

"It looks like a feast," Perseus says.

"Let's eat!" Hercules shouts.

"Wait," Jason says as screams are heard in the distance. "What about the harpies?"

A flock of harpies flies through the holes in the roof. They have the bodies of birds and the heads of women. Landing on the tables, they start digging in with their talons. Food flies everywhere.

"They are ruining supper!" Theseus shouts.

Just then, one of the harpies grabs a lump of mashes potatoes. She flings it at our heroes, smacking Odysseus in the face.

"Hey!" he shouts.

Then a watermelon lands on Hercules' head. **SPLAT!**

Theseus is pelted with grapes.

A bowl of gravy gets dumped all over Perseus.

"Food fight!" Jason shouts.

He grabs a bottle of ketchup. Squeezing it, he sprays one of the harpies.

**"EEEKKK!"** she screeches.

A harpy grabs a talonful of carrots and flings them at Jason. He ducks behind a table, and they **THUNK! THUNK! THUNK! THUNK!** into the wood.

Odysseus grabs a bottle of mustard. He sprays another one of the harpies.

**"AAAKKK!"** she screeches.

A harpy flies toward the heroes, trying to claw at them with her talons. But Perseus grabs a bottle of mayonnaise and sprays her in the face. She crashes into a table.

One harpy picks up a whole bowl of beef stew. She dumps it on Hercules' head. So he grabs bowl of dragon's breath peppers and starts winging them at her. They burst into flames as they hit the wall.

Back and forth they fight. The heroes squirt condiments at the harpies. The harpies fling mashed potatoes and vegetables back at the heroes.

Finally, when all the food has been ruined, the harpies let loose one final **SCREEECH!**

Then the harpies all fly up through the holes in the roof.

"What have you done?!" King Phineas yells at the heroes.

"We saved you from the harpies," Jason says.

"But look at this mess," the king says.

Soup pools on the floor. Lumps of mashed potatoes drip down the walls. The ceiling is covered in streaks of ketchup and mustard.

"You made a worse mess then those hags," the king yells. He picks up a broom and chases the heroes out of the castle.

"Get out! Get out!" he screams.

The heroes race back to their boat. As they shove off, Jason yells, "This why we should never stop for adventure!"

Then he lets loose a long, loud **FFFTTTHHHBBB!**

## CHAPTER FOUR

# DUNG MEN

The heroes continue on their quest. But Jason does not let them go ashore again—not until days later when they finally reach Colchis.

As the heroes tie up their rowboat, King Aeetes walks out to meet them. With him are several guards carrying long, pointy spears. Jason feels his tummy begin to rumble.

"Do you need to use the restroom?" Hercules asks.

"No," Jason whispers.

Then he lets loose a little **PFFFT!**

"I just need to belch," Jason adds, "from my back end."

As King Aeetes approaches, he scrunches up his nose.

"Did you come here just to fart?" he asks.

"No!" Jason says, embarrassed. "I am here to get my father's fleece back."

"Seriously?" King Aeetes asks. "That fleece is totally funky. It smells worse than the cloud of brown gas surrounding your boat."

"I still need it," Jason declares. "To prove that my father is king."

"Well, he lost it fair and square," says King Aeetes. "He said he could belch the entire alphabet and passed out on L-M-N-O-P."

"We could just take it from you," Hercules warns, as he flexes his biceps.

"I wouldn't try," Aeetes says. "It is guarded by a dragon."

"I will do anything to get the fleece back," Jason begs.

"Then come to my palace tomorrow," the king says. "I will have three tasks for you. Complete them, and you can have the fleece."

That night, Jason worries about the challenges King Aeetes will present to him tomorrow. As he worries, he **PFFFTS!**

"That smells worse than Ares' underwear," Hercules says.

"And he never washes them," Theseus adds.

"Hercules would know," Odysseus says.

"He was once dared to steal them," Perseus adds.

"I am just nervous about tomorrow's challenges," Jason says and then lets loose a *PTTTBBB!*

His friends all gasp and cover their noses.

Just then, a voice whispers in the night, "Maybe I can help."

Out of the shadows steps a woman. Her face is hidden under the hood of a robe.

"Who are you?" Jason asks.

"My name is Medea, and I am the king's daughter," the woman says. "I will help you, but only if you take that funky fleece away. My father likes to wear it around the house, and it smells worse than sweaty socks. No, worse than that, like the sweaty socks were barfed up by a giant slug and then flushed down the sewers of the Underworld. It smells horrible."

"But how?" Jason asks.

"Take these," she says, handing Jason a pair of gloves and a clothespin. "You will understand tomorrow."

The next morning, Jason and his friends go to find King Aeetes. He is standing outside his horse stables. Next to him is a giant ball of brown stinky stuff.

"Is that horse manure?" Perseus asks.

"Smells like it," Theseus says as he leans in for a big sniff.

Odysseus pokes the ball with his pinky and then licks the finger clean. "Tastes like it, too," he adds.

"It is, and it's for Jason's first tasks," King Aeetes says. "I want you to bring it up to that hill."

"But the smell!" Jason moans.

That is when he remembers the clothespin Medea gave him. He puts it on his nose.

"That's better," Jason says. "But I don't want to touch it."

And that is when he remembers the gloves Medea gave him. He quickly puts them on.

Then Jason pushes and rolls, shoves and heaves, the ball of dung up the hill. By the end he is covered in poo from head to toe. But at least our hero can't smell the mess, not like everyone else.

"Now what?" Jason asks.

"Spread it out over this field," King Aeetes says.

"Okay," Jason says grabbing a handful of manure. "But I really wish Medea would have given me a shovel."

Jason flings and tosses, throws and chucks the horse poop everywhere.

He is now more a mess than even before.

Everyone, including his friends, stands far, far away from him.

"That wasn't too difficult. Just smelly," Jason says. "What's my last challenge?"

"Now spread these all over the field," the kings says, handing Jason a small sack.

"What's in it?" he asks.

"My fingernails and toenail clippings," the king says.

"Ewww," Jason groans. Touching them is worse that digging into manure. They are covered in fungus!

But he does as the king asks. He tosses the toenail and fingernail clippings all about.

Once he's done, he turns to the king.

"Is that all?" Jason asks.

The king only smiles.

"You might want to turn back around," Theseus says to Jason.

"Yeah, like right now," Perseus adds.

Behind our hero, the ground begins to shake. It rumbles and quakes. Then a hand bursts forth. And another. And another. They are followed by heads and shoulders.

"Meet my dung men." The king laughs.

Nearly a dozen humanlike creatures crawl out of the earth.

"They look like turds with arms and legs," Perseus yells.

"And smell like it too," Theseus hollers.

"I wonder how they taste," Odysseus says.

"No time for that now," Hercules shouts. "Finally a battle!"

During all his friends' shouting, Jason's stomach begins to warble and burble.

And just as a dung man is about to sneak up behind him and clobber our hero, he lets loose a loud **PTTTHHHBBB!**

His butt-bomb sends the dung man flying backward. The beast crumbles apart as it crashes to the ground.

"Do that again!" Perseus shouts.

As another dung man raises his arm to club Jason, he turns and ducks. He lets out more fanny thunder. **PFFFTTTHHH!!!** The gas blasts the creature to pieces.

"I think I might have to wipe after that one," Jason says with a grin.

Then his friends join in.

Hercules pulls out his pooper-scooper. He scoops out chunk after chunk from dung men, flinging manure all over.

Perseus makes poo kabobs by running his wooden spear through two dung men.

Theseus slices and dices dung men with his trident.

Odysseus pulls out his slingshot and pelts the dung men. *THWIP! THWIP!* Rocks zip right through them.

Jason lets loose one final cheek squeaker *PFFFTTTBBB!!* The last dung man explodes, and hunks of poo rain down and splatter everyone.

Our heroes are victorious!

"So where is my father's fleece?" Jason demands of King Aeetes.

## CHAPTER FIVE

# INTO THE DRAGON'S NOSTRILS

"You will find the fleece in there," King Aeetes says, pointing to a strange-looking cave.

"But where is the dragon that guards the fleece?" Jason asks.

"Oh, I made that up," Aeetes says with a wink.

Inside the cavern, greenish stalagmites rise up from the ground. Oozing stalactites hang from the ceiling. A river of thick yellow goo flows from deep within. And a warm, stanky wind rushes out.

As Jason stands before the entrance, Medea walks over to him. She hands him a small package, so nobody else will see.

"You'll need this to get out once you find the fleece," Medea whispers.

"Thanks," Jason says, and then he enters the cave. A long tunnel leads into the dark.

From above, yellowish-green slime **DRiP DRiP DROPS** onto the ground.

Jason walks through puddles of the sticky ooze. At one point, his left boot is pulled off with a **SMUCK!** and sticks in the goo. Then his right boot is yanked off.

He walks through the cave with hot, sticky ooze **SQUISHING** between his toes.

The farther he walks, the hotter the air gets. He starts to sweat.

Then the tunnel opens into a large cavern.

Jason looks around. He is amazed at what he sees—and also slightly disgusted.

Red veins cover the walls. The floor is covered in yellow muck, so thick he can hardly walk. Above him hangs a pinkish-gray mass about the size of his rowboat. It dangles from more of the red veins.

Jason is about to reach up to touch it, when he spies the object of his quest. On the far wall hangs his father's fleece.

Jason runs over and pulls it down.

"Ew, it does smell totally funky!" He coughs as he pulls it over his shoulders.

Jason turns to leave, but he is stuck in the muck covering the floor. That is when he remembers the package Medea gave him.

He opens it to find a glowing red pepper. It almost looks as if it were on fire.

"A dragon's breath pepper," Jason whispers.

Jason winds up. He tosses the pepper up at the gray mass hanging from the ceiling.

The pepper explodes in a ball of flame. The mass begins to wriggle and jerk and bounce around.

The red veins on the wall throb.

The muck on the floor bubbles.

Then Jason hears a loud *"AHHH!"*

He covers his ears as another *"AHHH!"* fills the cave.

That is followed by a deafening *"CHHHOOO!!!"*

A blast of air knocks Jason off his feet. He is sent tumbling down the tunnel. He bounces off oozing stalactites. He pinballs off sticky stalagmites. He splashes through the river of ooze.

Then he is shot out of the cavern!

But it is actually not a cavern after all.

As Jason flies through the air, he sees a large dragon rearing up its head. It is sneezing and shooting snot and fire from its nostrils.

Just as Jason realizes he was crawling around in a dragon's nostril, he **SMACKS!** into a rocky cliff.

That is followed by a loud **SPAT!** as he is covered in smoky, oozing snot.

"I can't move!" he yells to his friends, who come running to help.

The dragon's mucus is as thick as glue.

His friends have to tug and pull, yank and pry him off the wall.

"I don't know what smells worse," Perseus says.

"Your farts," Hercules says.

"Or burning boogers," Theseus says.

"I know what taste worse," Odysseus says, licking his finger.

"Hurry up!" Theseus shouts. "King Aeetes does not look happy."

The king, with several guards and their long, pointy spears, race toward Jason and his friends.

Our heroes take off, running to their rowboat. They all jump in, and the boat lurches forward as Jason begins to sing, *"Row! Row! Row your boat!"*

The trip home is uneventful. Jason does not let his friends go ashore for any reason.

He doesn't let them go for food. Or if they need to go to the bathroom. And definitely not if they see monsters or beasts.

Back in Iolcus, Jason barges into the throne room. He holds up the fleece for all to see.

Instead of pointing their spears at him, the guards wrinkle their noses in disgust.

"I have the fleece," Jason shouts. "Release my father!"

"Anything, if you just put that away." Pelias coughs. "It smells like a loogey from the nostrils of a dragon."

Guards rush off to get Jason's father. They return with the king moments later.

"The throne is yours again, father," Jason says. "And I brought back the fleece for you."

Jason's father turns green in disgust as Jason holds out the fleece to him.

"I'd rather go back to jail than wear that," the kings says.

"But you need it to be king," Jason says.

"Son, I purposely lost that belching contest so King Aeetes would take the fleece," his father says. "I hated wearing that funky smelling thing."

"But the king must wear it," Jason says.

"Then you be king," his father says, pushing the totally funky fleece back at Jason.

Jason pulls the fleece over his shoulders.

"I am the new king of Iolcus!" he announces.

Everyone if the room bows. Some out of respect to the new king. Others, because the stench of the fleece is making them gag and cough. And vomit.

"I think I'm gonna be sick," Hercules says.

"I may throw up," Perseus says.

"Race you to the bathroom," Odysseus says.

"Last one there is a funky fleece,"
Theseus says.

# THE REAL MYTH

In myths, Jason was the son of King Aeson, ruler of the city of Iolcus. When he was a child, his uncle Pelias took the throne from the king and had Aeson imprisoned. Jason escaped and was raised by Chiron, a wise Centaur who taught him how to fight.

When he was an adult, Jason went to get his father's kingdom back. But the only way King Pelias would give the throne back is if Jason found the Golden Fleece. This magical hide was from a golden ram that once belonged to Jason's ancestors. It would give Jason the right to the kingdom.

For his quest, Jason asked for help. Famous heroes from across the land joined him. They included Hercules, the strongest person in the world. He also had a mighty ship built, the *Argos*, which gave the heroes their name, Argonauts.

Jason and the Argonauts sailed to Colchis, a land ruled by King Aeetes. The king did not want to give up the fleece, so he challenged Jason to several deadly tasks. To complete them, the king's daughter, Medea, offered to help him, but only if he would marry her.

Jason was able to take the Golden Fleece from King Aeetes and then returned to Iolcus. He eventually became the city's ruler.

# GLOSSARY

cyclops (SYE-klahps)—a one-eyed giant

dingy (DING-ee)—small, but also a small boat

fleece (FLEESS)—wool from a sheep

harpy (HAR-pee)—a creature in myth that has the body of a bird and the head of a woman

loogey (LOO-gee)—another word for snot or boogers

mucus (MYOO-kuhss)—also another word for snot or boogers

quest (KWEST)—a journey made to find something or to perform a task

rudder (RUHD-ur)—part of a boat that is used to control which direction it goes

stalactite (stuh-LAK-tite)—a structure that hangs down like an icicle

stalagmite (stuh-LAG-mite)—a cone-shaped structure that rises up from the ground

stern (STERN)—the back of a boat or ship

# AUTHOR

Blake Hoena grew up in central Wisconsin, where he wrote stories about robots conquering the moon and trolls lumbering around the woods behind his parents' house. He now lives in St. Paul, Minnesota, and continues to make up stories about things like space aliens and superheroes, and he has written more than 70 chapter books and graphic novels for children.

# ILLUSTRATOR

Ivica Stevanovic is illustrator, comic artist and graphic designer. He has published a huge number of illustrations in schoolbooks and picture books. Apart from working on illustrations for children's books, Ivica draws comics, and his specialty is graphic novels. His best-known graphic novel is *Kindly Corpses*. Ivica lives with his wife Milica and their two daughters Katarina and Teodora in Veternik (Serbia).

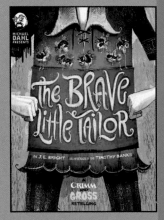
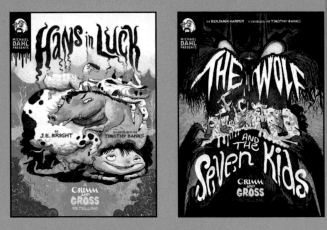